Winter Sky

Stories for the Season

Shelley Thompson

Vagrant Press

Vagrant Press is an imprint of
Nimbus Publishing Limited
3660 Strawberry Hill Street, Halifax, NS, B3K 5A9
(902) 455-4286 nimbus.ca

Nimbus Publishing is based in Kjipuktuk, Mi'kma'ki, the traditional territory of the Mi'kmaq People.

This story is a work of fiction. Names, characters, incidents, and places, including organizations and institutions, either are the product of the author's imagination or are used fictitiously.

Printed and bound in Canada

NB1787

Editor: Whitney Moran
Design and interior illustrations: Bee Stanton

Library and Archives Canada Cataloguing in Publication

Title: Winter sky : stories for the season / Shelley Thompson.
Names: Thompson, Shelley (Actress), author.
Identifiers: Canadiana (print) 20250217945 | Canadiana (ebook) 2025022464X | ISBN 9781774714706 (softcover
ISBN 9781774714713 (EPUB)
Subjects: LCGFT: Short stories. | LCGFT: Christmas fiction.
Classification: LCC PS8639.H6397 W56 2025 | DDC C813/.6—dc23

Nimbus Publishing acknowledges the financial support for its publishing activities from the Government of Canada, the Canada Council for the Arts, and from the Province of Nova Scotia. We are pleased to work in partnership with the Province of Nova Scotia to develop and promote our creative industries for the benefit of all Nova Scotians.

Contents

A Beakful of Berry 1

The Thing of It Is 11

December 1945 25

Bowls of Cheer 39

A Goat's Christmas Carol 49

A Wheel of Cheese 61

Angel in Tompkins Square 73

The Compass 93

Winter Sky 125

Acknowledgements 131

A Beakful of Berry

A Reflection

We all need moments in our lives when we feel like the hero of our own stories. When our derring-do, our weighed and wise choices, our empathy and openness, mark us as interesting, worthy, considerate. Human.

In early December years ago, a week after the first major winter storm of the season, I was walking my dog through the beautiful rural community where my child went to middle school. A ramble that took me around a lake, past farmland and woodlots, over streams and up hills that provided, at the top, a view of the grey-green Northumberland Strait in the distance.

I never did that walk without counting my blessings: my health, my family's health, and my dog's health (and her sheer joy and exuberance). Tibbit was my first dog: a dog with huge energy and a beautiful soul. Because of her, I saw things I'd never otherwise see. Metaphorically, as well as literally.

This morning was no different, though it was colder and brighter than the week before. As she so often did, Tibbit bounded into the bush, where she flushed out a robin. What was different this time was that, with uncharacteristic calm, the hundred pounds of gold and black *maybe Labrador*—or *maybe mastiff*, *maybe shepherd*—nosed so slowly and delicately through the snow toward the bird, forcing it to back awkwardly into a tangle of brush. There it sat, its sweet red breast heaving. Too exhausted, it seemed, to attempt escape.

Tibbit watched it, perplexed and indecisive. She turned to me with a question on her face. I wasn't entirely sure what the question was, but it wasn't "Shall I eat it?" which was generally her first response to anything she'd found. (That's the *maybe Labrador* part.)

I had a moment of quandary: I was a distance from my vehicle, and then a half-hour drive from home. I'd have to hold the bird while driving winter roads that required some concentration even when *not* trying to cradle an injured creature. The robin's attention was fixed, understandably, on Tibbit, who had, very unusually, sat down quietly at my feet. Then, the bird turned its dark eyes to me.

I wasn't imagining it; the bird was making a mute appeal to Tib and me. I reached slowly into the snarl of rose bushes and hawthorn; the bird didn't flinch or struggle. I got him between my bulky mitts, opened my coat, and holding him gently against my chest, I headed off with Tib hard on my heels. In the car, Tibbit, always a restless passenger, rested her head on my shoulder, as still as she'd ever been. Usually, she'd circle and settle, circle and settle, stand and sit. But now she worked hard to keep her balance, back feet on the back seat, front legs between the two front seats, and head as close to the robin tucked into my coat as she could get. We drove like that, Tib's breath hot in my ear, home.

Living near Antigonish there was a woman, a painter and writer, who was something of a legend for her care and understanding of animals, and in particular, birds. Linda Johns and her partner, Mac, celebrated the wild things around them every day: feeding a family of porcupines at their window box, refereeing the occasional dust-up between those porcupines and a curious raccoon or squirrel. Their home and garden provided sanctuary for all sorts of creatures, and they were the first people you'd call when you found a wounded bird.

They urged me to bring my robin along. When I arrived, Linda had prepared a selection of delicacies to tempt him: fresh clean water with a hint of berry on the side, something grainy, and the treat of treats apparently—mealworms. At first the robin didn't respond to the drops of water dribbled down his beak, then, mixed with a drop of berry juice, he did. The beak opened a crack, then a little more: enough to clutch a mealworm. With delight, Linda moved the robin to a covered spot where her "nurse bird," a starling saved a few years before, approached to investigate...and chat. The starling, Starr, chirruped and trilled directly to the robin, and came and went while I watched. Starr knew her job. She provided a kind of bird-human connection, letting the robin know that he was in a place of sanctuary: a place where he could get well, get strong, then get back to his own life.

I left my robin in safe hands. I'd had an adventure; I'd been a hero, albeit briefly, and my story would end, had already ended, happily.

The next morning, I called to check the progress of my former charge. He had not survived the night.

Mac sounded as distressed as I felt. He and Linda had thought the robin was doing well, making progress. Jumping between branches, chatting with Starr. Then suddenly, silence. When they investigated, he'd retreated into the bushes, Starr quietly chatting and, it seemed, offering support. But then, he died.

When Mac went to pick him up, he was shocked: the robin had clearly starved to death. Nothing but bone, and not saved in time.

I got off the phone, then spent a good part of my day in tears. Why, when there were so many more things to weep about, was this so affecting?

I'd carried that damaged creature to his sanctuary imagining I could save him, or at least help save him. And I discovered, as I wafted weepily around my house, that my tears were only partly for my robin. They were for me, and my disappointment in failing at a time when I needed badly to do tangible good, somewhere. Somehow.

This was taking place during early December, those weeks that race into the festive season, when we're surrounded by largesse and excess, excitement and joy, anticipation, and for me, dread. I'd not been looking forward to the celebration of the large day and then the New Year to come, with its forward motion, potential for change, and another reshape of The Future.

The world felt bleak. The Syrian war was ever-present in the news, and the coming celebration in our town, which was a bastion of Catholicism (I'm not a Catholic), felt particularly false and forced. I remember trying that year to (gently) share with my old-soul child some of my complex feelings about the holiday. What Christmases long past had meant, and what I'd always hoped they might come to mean to our family, careful to disguise my dismay and sense of culpability for perpetuating a season sodden with acquisitiveness.

I wasn't The Grinch, I just wanted a different sort of focus. What though? *Expecting* and *giving* and *receiving* in a different spirit—one I wasn't sure I understood or could demonstrate myself.

The conversations I had with my child during this time felt profound. The little bird made us think about life and death. About home. About loneliness. About the acceptance of one stranger—Starr the nurse bird—for another of its kind, but differently feathered. About family. Christmas put a burning glass, more than ever this year, on what we had, and what others didn't. The complexity and responsibility: to teach compassion and clarity and kindness, and leave out fear and pain. Round and round I went. *Perseverating.* All this guilt and sadness for the whole world, the need to do the right thing, embodied in one tiny, starved bird.

In my outsized response to the robin, I recognized a struggle with loss and frustration of a different stripe, activated by the helplessness of these particular domestic circumstances at this moment in history: so very *hands on* to save the bird; so, *we can do it*!, and then shocker, *no we can't*. Beyond that red-and-brown bird, so many I couldn't help, who'd never know or care that I'd lost sleep over them.

But if I could have saved the robin, I'd have done something. I grieved, as much as his death, my inability to save him, and change the future.

Finding, and losing, the robin was a tiny parenthesis of loss and helplessness in a fortunate life. My dear Tib, with her sweet curiosity, who'd brought me so many lessons, had now brought me this. A Christmas blessing of guilt and insomnia. The gift of sitting wakeful with myself in solidarity with those who, unlike my robin, didn't have the briefest sanctuary in which to enjoy a beakful of berry water.

The Thing of It Is

Oh, Christmas. We remember what we had. Who we've lost. How we ache. We remember disasters and triumphs and the deepest, sweetest friends, telling the hardest truths.

I had a carpenter once, Cob. Cob the Carp, everyone called him. He was famous for his carpentry and was the unofficial mayor in our tiny town—which, by the way, really pissed the *official* mayor off. Whenever election time rolled around, the official mayor, who'd held that office for ten years when we arrived from away (and went on to hold it for twelve more), would meet Cob in the street—I was with him once—and pump his hand, and ask him about the building trade and say he must be mad busy, then look relieved when Cob stopped shaking his hand but kept holding it. Cob would say "S'okay, Ronny." (The mayor was called Ronald MacDonald. Really.) "S'okay," he'd say, "I'm not running this time.

Next time m'be." And Mayor Ron would breathe relief at the gift of another term, courtesy of Cob, and move along the main street glad-handing as he went.

Cob turned to me that time and gave a wicked wink with one of his button eyes. And by the way, Cob's last name was MacDonald too. He and the mayor were almost certainly related. Probably sixty-five percent of our town was made up of MacDonalds, and everyone seemed to have a nickname, because there were only so many Christian names to go around. I knew six John A. MacDonalds, and they ended up being called Zip MacDonald and Cash MacDonald and Red MacDonald and even Boss MacDonald. So you could know who folks were actually gossiping about.

Anyway.

Cob is a MacDonald, or was. He's dead now, the darling man. Sudden, but of course it wasn't. He was a smoker. He smoked too much. He smoked when he wasn't talking and he talked a lot but he managed to smoke a lot too, so it was cancer that got him. And though mostly it was cigarettes, sometimes it was cig-arillos, those awful-smelling mini cigars? So, yeah, a variety of combustibles, predominately a very famous and very strong cigarette, beloved of cowboys and bloody-minded women, I'm told, and the most foul cigarette he could get. And then, during his treatment, he stopped tobacco and started on pot. But when he was working on a property—and I came to recognize this was a real stress response; when you saw this as a home owner, you got pretty anxious wondering what the heck he'd found now—occasionally he'd pull out a pipe. Hence, Cob. As in, "corn cob."

He had small, shiny black eyes, and loads of curly white hair, so "a corn cob pipe and two button eyes"—was that how it went? Anyway, I wondered for a long time why he wasn't called Frosty except it turns out there was another Frosty McDonald, only a Mc not a Mac, and much older, but also, Cob was anything but frosty. He was warm and loving, and when he was working on your place, your place was *his* place, and everything mattered, a lot, so when that pipe came out, everyone's blood pressure went up.

When he was sucking on that pipe, he wasn't talking. He was *looking* with laser intensity at whatever was plaguing him, and he'd stand, silently sucking, and nodding, willing the wall or the pipe or the brickwork or whatever it was to explain itself. He was listening profoundly to his collaborator: the house. And then he'd turn back to you with a solution. Or condolences. And he'd have one last pull on his pipe, blow out a long plume, considering *you* now, wondering if you could absorb, accept, or endure what he needed to impart, and he'd drawl gently, looking unwaveringly at you, "Ya know, the thing of it is..."

"The thing of it is" was rarely good news. Once in a very blue moon, perhaps. Or sometimes it was one thing *evolving* into something more positive through a bold plan of attack. A creative solution to a knotty little snag. Something wrapped into a whole new idea or daring choice. Cob and I both loved buildings and bending them to our wills. Sometimes "the thing of it is" was delivered in discovering a previously unimagined way to solve a headache-y puzzle that was keeping us awake at night. So, when either Cob or I—or both of us—would wake and say to ourselves or the person lying next to us, "Ah...the thing of is!," it was a practical and aesthetically pleasing solution. Coming from Cob though, discoveries, good or bad, were always delicately delivered, removing responsibility from everyone and everything, except *the* thing. The thing of it is.

Like Christmas.

Over all the years we knew Cob, we must have had a half-dozen Christmases when he was actively working on our house, and many more when he was just there because by then, we'd absorbed each other. One Christmas—the first pandemic Christmas—because of the chaos in the building trade and the supply chain, the massive reno he was doing on our kitchen had gone on for nine months, and by October, the seventh month, I started providing a birthday cake for the project on the fifteenth of each month. We both had a sweet tooth and it was as good an excuse as any to indulge it during our afternoon tea breaks: Cob, from hammering on my house, mine from hammering on my keyboard. We'd sing happy birthday to whatever he was working on—the countertops, or the tiling—eat our cake, and get back to work.

Cob had opinions about Christmas that he was happy to share.

"The thing of it is," said Cob, "*everything* happens at Christmas. The drains back up; your mother-in-law comes; your friends get drunk and embarrassing and you realize you never really liked them, they don't like you, and neither of you know why you're friends; your wife tells you she's pregnant or she's having an affair, or both"—I looked at him and wondered—"and it's always right before the turkey goes on the table and everything goes to shit. Christmas is...well, fuck."

And he went silent.

It was the only time I heard him say *fuck*, and it was not long before he died, and it was Christmas. Christmas Day, actually, and the basement had water coming in.

Cob wasn't at our house for the seeping wall in our basement. We aren't those people who call on Christmas expecting service. Cob was at our house because, after twenty years of helping us create a home from the ground up and watching our family grow and making our children his, he was joining us for Christmas dinner. Our kids said we had our own Santa. And it was true, because sometimes in the run-up to Christmas, Cob did a little moonlighting as St. Nick, growing out a huge white beard, making the rounds of the local schools' winter fairs, and even, during one beautiful, almost divine rapprochement, joining Mayor Ron for a carol service and town tree lighting.

And that beard. It was a marvel how fast he could grow it. We'd joke it was like one of those dolls where you pressed a button on her back and you could change the length of her hair. We'd say, "Who d'ya get to press the button on your back?" And then we'd always feel a little bad, because as long as we'd known Cob, he'd never had a someone who might push that imaginary button. We felt bad, but also smug. Poor Cob.

But this particular Christmas was different. Cob was less of a Santa, less upright. Less hearty and no cigarettes. He listened more, talked and laughed less. When he talked, he coughed. This Christmas our kids came home with a secret they'd shared with each other, but not with us—one belonging to our daughter. That was the point and the pain: our daughter was home from university for the first time, and it was the reason my husband and I were...ya know. Not at our Christmas best.

Christmas, Cob started up again, was someone's idea of a joke. Hell, masquerading as peace and joy and love. Domestic combustion masquerading—when Cob got hold of a word or phrase, he used the shit out of it—as the warm glow of a cozy hearth with slippers and hot chocolate and... He waved his pipe, getting a little animated. He had his pipe out because he'd discovered a crack in our foundation, which explained the water seeping into the basement where our children were sleeping on their Christmas vacation, so yeah. Cob's pipe was very much in evidence. He'd brought me to look at the foundation at the bottom of our chimney stack, first shovelling the fresh snow away from the house, because my husband and I were about to tear each other apart—respectfully, because it was Christmas, but still viscerally—and because he loved us and we loved him, he was trying to avert, or at least postpone that, until after Boxing Day when the kids were gone.

It was grinding to the end of a bumpy and uncomfortable year. Our son had quit university—his fourth year, not even two weeks into the fall term—deciding none of it was for him, and had gone back to his summer tree-planting camp to finish out their season. Then he moved into a squat—a squat! Who knew there were still squats! Wasn't that an eighties thing?—in the city with people we'd never met, and were, frankly, afraid of. And our daughter. Well, the tree-planting and squat paled.

Our daughter had grown less and less communicative over her first term, then come home and gone to her room. Their room—I'm trying. They came home and went to their room and stayed there. Their hair was shorn and, I discovered when I went in on Christmas morning to wake her—them—they had a tattoo. Not huge, not ugly, but. A tattoo. She—shit, they—knew how we—well only me, apparently, that is part of the reason my husband wanted to eviscerate me, because I kept ascribing characteristics and views to him that were in fact only mine—she/they knew we/I hated tattoos, and had still gone ahead and got one. On their own body. How dare she. They.

On that morning, Christmas morning, *Family Perfection Day*, that choice by my child to do with their body what they wanted to, felt like, and was presented by me to all my family (poor choice, looking back) as, a betrayal of a formerly close and, according to all my friends, enviable relationship. With a child who told me everything. Who actually didn't, and hadn't for some time. There was a lot I'd discovered in the last few days that I didn't know. Starting with the most simple of facts.

The framing: Cob's definition.

She wasn't her. That is, she wasn't my daughter anymore. She was, they were, someone I didn't know, though now, the thing of it is, I do and think I always did, actually, and for years I'd ignored it because I thought it didn't matter or wasn't my business (close!), or maybe I couldn't name it. Or wouldn't. Jeez, though. It was just them.

But standing outside with Cob, who was dying by then only we didn't really know, staring at the foundation with the crack that was seeping and threatening the structure of our house—except Cob had identified it, so maybe we'd be fine—with the Christmas-scented smoke from our fireplace, the snow in the air, the ten-year-old across the road shrieking in delight at their new puppy, all those oh-so-Christmassy tropes, my heart was breaking. Maybe exploding. With fear but also with such inexpressible love and—this surprised me—pride in my child, who was, had always been, so like themselves and so like their brother and who wanted, more than anything, only to be who they knew they were. But I wanted what I wanted.

A solid, beautiful house. A simple family, different from the one in which I'd grown up, unencumbered by...complexity.

Still silent, Cob sucked on his pipe. Then he turned to me and said, 'The thing of it is, she's—sorry, it's they, right? they—they're okay. They're here. They're waiting to be happy. But they can't, right, they can't be happy, till things are safe and solid around them, right? The thing of it is, angel"—he always called me angel; ironically, I'm absolutely sure—"The thing of it is, all you've ever wanted is for them to be happy. Not like"—and this wasn't a word he used and it was an effort—"superficially. Like, *happy*."

And then, Cob looked up at the chimney with the scented smoke escaping in an indeterminate papal grey—who knew what was going on in there—and he squeezed his left eye closed and took a deep breath in, and I knew he was doing this thing he'd told me about to control anxiety. A big, sweet, smart, confident man like him, taking deep breaths. He'd told me: close your left eye, then look up and breathe deep for thirty seconds. This kind of short-circuits the anxiety bit of your brain and stops it taking hold. He never told me who told him that, or why he'd needed to find out. But anyway, he was doing that.

I watched the stillness of his big face, half hidden by the massive seasonal white hedge, breathing, breathing, coughing, then breathing.

He loved our youngest. He'd taught them to hammer straight; to turn a screw, walk away, come back, and turn it again; and, most important, to measure twice, cut once. A principle I'd seen my child employ in so much of their life. They were meticulous and non-judgemental and that was not my parenting or even my balanced, quiet husband's. That was Cob. Cob, with no children, with no family. Cob who was effortlessly cool and easy. Measure twice, cut once, Cob.

So Cob was still looking up, breathing and maybe counting to thirty or a hundred or whatever, but on that still, still Christmas Day—even the shrieking monster-child across the street and their new puppy were silent now—Cob was helping me build something again. Something to make that day, the next day, the weeks and months and years ahead, more solid and steadfast. Sheltering. Something I could lean on and know it would withstand any kind of storm.

He dropped his head, dropped the hand that was covering his left eye, and said, "The thing of it is, it's only a day. And they are the darling person they always were. Give them what they want for Christmas."

I looked at him. "What? What's the thing of it?!"

He shrugged, looked at the crack in our foundation, tapped out his pipe, and tucking it carefully in his coat, headed for the door.

I followed.

Now, every Christmas—which I rage against, then measure *twice* and cut, or pour, or wrap *once*—when I look at my second son, I know exactly, but imperfectly, what the thing of it is.

December 1945

I kissed my brother and saw his eyes fill as he turned away, leaving me at the altar on my groom's right arm. Ron's good hand trembled as he reached for me, and catching Bill's eye, he pressed the tiny glass button into my palm. I closed my fist tightly around that secret, then opened it wide to see the talisman glinting in my palm as the minister began: "Dearly Beloved."

The night before, excitement keeping her awake, my young niece Beth had asked for a story.

Out of your mouth, Beth commanded, a secret you've never told before this special night.

A secret good, or a secret bad? I'd replied.

Do you have a secret bad? Young Beth was horrified and thrilled at the thought.

Everyone has a secret bad. I had many, but not the sort my little Beth had in mind. My secrets were stories: moving pictures that come alive in my cinema mind in unguarded moments. Stories and sounds of the war I'd been determined to help win, where, as a Nursing Sister working from dirt-floored tents too close to the Front, I'd seen and heard far more than I'd ever tell anyone, least of all this sweet-cheeked eight-year-old.

But I had the button. Or rather, the story of the button. And so I'd told her that.

Her father, I told my niece, hadn't always been the gentle, patient teacher Beth knew. Once, Billy's sole purpose in life had been to torment his little sister; to tease, and chase, and dare me to distraction. And on that December day long ago, when I was exactly the age Beth was now, the teasing and daring led to a lesson neither of us would ever forget.

Mother had sent us into a snow-white day, through the village and over the river to Aunty May's house. She'd entrusted us with collecting the dress our aunt would wear on her wedding day—Christmas Eve, a week away—for mother to finish some fine embroidery. An important job for Billy, twelve then, and me, eight.

Winter had come early that year, with the river ice setting hard by early December. The first skating had already taken place the week before, though Billy and I had been forbidden. Too soon! said our father, who knew about ice, hauling timber across that same river with his two huge Clydesdales, but never, he said, before at least mid-January.

Now, days after watching our friends skate the edge of the river, we were crunching through banks of snow, the sugar-candy crust breaking with every step. The weather had been capricious: mountains of dry snow, below freezing for over a week, then a tease of two or three warm days, another cold snap, another two or three warm. Even as we walked, the bright sun covered itself with a layer of cloud.

As we walked, we fought.

Billy wanted to go over the river, or said he did, teasing me terrified at the prospect of breaking the rules. Then he said I'd have no flowers to carry at Aunty's wedding—flowers don't come till spring, he said.

They do, I said.

Don't, said Billy.

Do, I said. Mom had promised I'd carry flowers. It was a wedding; of course there would be flowers!

What would you know about weddings, Billy persisted—you've never been to one.

Well, I knew anyways, I said, and what's more, I know what flowers I'll have at *my* wedding! Someday.

Ha! was Billy's response, your wedding! Ha! And he laughed and rolled in the snow. Who, he asked, would ever marry you?

Someone, I replied.

Yah, someone. Someone has to love you to marry you.

Someone will, I said. I was almost crying now. Someone does. Mom does. Aunty does.

Ha! Billy chortled again. You can't marry Mom. Or Aunty.

I know, I said. I'm not so dumb. Someone will love me. You're a bully, I told my brother. Someone does love me!

Now I was crying, and Billy knew he'd gone just too far.

Alright alright. Maybe someone will love you. Maybe. Someday. Stop it now. We're nearly there.

And we were. I wiped my eyes on the backs of my mitts, and when Aunty opened her door, with the beautiful smile everyone said had made our nearly-uncle fall in love with her, I was fine again. Aunty May, Mother said, knew just how to spoil a child. And Mother was right, for there was our favourite: johnny-cake, slathered in maple syrup. And for me, a promise, given with a hug, of flowers to carry at the wedding.

Before wrapping the gown we'd come for in brown paper, Auntie May spread it out to show us: lace like spiders' webs on the sleeves; tiny, fine stitching in the hem; a row of diamond-like glass buttons right down the back. In the sunny Sunday afternoon parlour they caught and threw the light, scattering rainbows every-where. Even Billy looked impressed. Pretty fancy, his grudging compliment.

We were full to bursting of johnnycake as we set out to retrace our steps home. The afternoon was darker now and far warmer than the day before, which had been warm enough. Now, the clouds were black and threatening something, and Billy decided he didn't want to be out in whatever it was.

When we reached the fork that meant a choice of the town road or the river way, which was shorter, Billy veered towards the river.

Hey, I said, we can't go that way. Mom said.

Baby, said my brother. Mom said, Mom said. It's quicker. Look at the storm coming. Do you want to be caught in it?

And as if to prove his point, great, oversized raindrops started to fall.

Are you coming? He stood, legs apart, arms crossed, while I shifted from foot to foot, hugging the parcel of the precious wedding dress, wishing I was home.

Mom said not across the ice. We have to go back over the bridge.

Mom's not here, is she. She'll never know.

Billy! Mom said! I don't want to go 'cross the ice.

Well, said Billy, go on then. You go around the long looong way, and I'll go home the short way and get my dinner first.

You just had lunch, I said. Piggy, piggy, piggy.

Don't matter. I'm hungry anyway, he said, turning away, and I want to get home quick. You go home over the bridge.

By myself? I looked up at the green-black sky. I hated when my brother did this, but as he turned to leave, I knew I couldn't bear the idea of the town road on my own, in the gathering gloom. I followed him, miserable, to the edge of the river where he inspected the ice.

Finally, he settled on a spot. Here, he said. Looks thick as can be. Come on.

Wait! I said. You take the dress. So Billy grabbed the parcel and set off across the river, turning to jump and bounce and watch as I picked my way across. Come on, he shouted. It won't break. It's winter. Just walk, don't be so stupid.

Stupid rankled. I might be small, I might be scared, I might be weaker than Billy, but I knew I wasn't stupid. I stamped my foot.

I'M NOT STUPID, I shouted to my brother, and the river and the sky. I'M NOT. And you're a bully and I don't even love you.

Well, called Billy, from nearly the other shore, we're quits then, 'cause I don't love you.

And then, where I had stamped my foot, the ice, slowly at first, began a kind of webbing. Like the lace on the dress, I thought. One thread connecting to another, and another. The ice was splintering and I saw I'd stepped on a piece that had water on one side, and then the other, and a fountain of water leapt through a crack like a creature. The ice shuddered and now I could feel the river running beneath my feet, cold and black, a gap widening as I watched. It was like I was inside a dream, watching myself from far away. Seconds, dressed as minutes, then days, seemed to pass: finally, I screamed.

Billy turned, his face shocked and afraid, but now he stood just too far away, a rushing black chasm growing between us.

Oh! Now what, now what! I cried.

Jump! he shouted. You have to jump! His voice was breaking as he stretched himself to the edge of the ice. I'll catch you. I will. I will.

And so, I jumped.

I was forever in the air—the same dream holding me up—then, suddenly, I was looking through thick, black water.

I could see only the jagged outline of broken ice as I fought with my clothes, pushing my hair from my eyes and scrabbling through water thick as jelly, choked with junks of ice, towards...something. Something white, floating. Floating, then sinking towards me.

I grabbed and hung onto the white. First, a lot of it in my hand, then less and less as the river pulled it from me, like a vicious tug-of-war. Then, nothing left but a tiny, hard moment of *something* stinging my frozen fingers. Finally, wanting nothing more than to suck a deep breath into my straining lungs, my head broke the surface, and Billy was pulling at me, and I was climbing and clawing and lying on the ice. I was crying, but Billy wasn't calling me a crybaby.

Somehow, we managed to clamber up the bank. Our teeth chattering, Billy clutched the wedding dress in a soggy bundle under his arm as he tried to drag me, limp and heavy with icy water, up the slippery bank. And in my stiff fingers, a tiny glass button.

We headed for the closest lights. The sky was nighttime-black now, the rain coming in sheets. Billy was quiet, and I realized my brother was crying.

Billy? I said.

Janey, he said, I'm so sorry. Here. Put on my coat.

Then you'll freeze, I said.

I deserve to freeze, he said, Oh, Janey, I'm sorry. And look at Aunty May's dress. Torn.

Only a little, I said. But see. This button. That's all I had hold of. But I pulled it right off.

I was shivering. I'm so cold, I said. Quick. Let's get to McLaren's. I pointed to the lights.

Where? said Billy.

Ronnie McLaren's. I was shaking worse now.

How d'ya know that, asked Billy, and he hugged me closer.

Because, I said. He loves me.

Does he? said Billy.

And then: So do I. I love you, Janey. And I'm sorry.

And we knocked at the door and only Ronnie, who loved me, was home. Everyone else had gone to a Christmas concert. So we got our wet things off, curled up by the fire, and Ronnie telephoned over to Aunty May, hoping she hadn't gone to the concert, careful not to say too much on the party line. She came in a hurry, by the road, and made some hot chocolate for us and took the dress to be washed, and never told our mother. When I told my aunty about the button, she cried a little and closed my hand over it and told me, Keep it.

And that's the secret. Your dad's, Ronnie's, Aunty May's, and my secret. And now, yours.

A secret good, said little Beth, and a secret bad. You nearly died, but Daddy saved you. Well, the button saved you. That, she said, was the secret good. And that was Uncle Ronnie!

It was. It is. And that was the end of the story and bedtime for Beth.

For me, though, it had been the beginning of a story. The love story of a boy growing into a soldier and a girl grown into a nurse. A soldier so badly wounded he was hardly recognizable; helped back to health by the girl from home, who pushed a glass button into his hand on the night she found him, and told him, Hold this. It will save you. It will. And we will marry on Christmas Eve.

He'd held it in his one good hand, and a tear traced a path through the blood and dirt around his ragged mouth, where now, as the minister finished and the music began, I saw a smile.

Standing in the church with my family gathered around me on this Christmas Eve, I remembered the way the ice had moved under my feet. And as the music swelled, I felt the church floor give, just for a moment, like that ice; like the dirt floor in the field hospital had trembled when I heard a name I knew and moved across that canvas cave to what I was afraid to find.

And now I knew—having been so near death, having seen so much death—that nothing would ever be solid again. All one could hold on to was the button of love, throwing the light from the Christmas candles all around us in tiny, magic rainbows.

Bowls of Cheer

"That horse has thrown another shoe."

"How many feet does that horse have, John? That's the sixth shoe in a month!"

Little Marta ran to the door where our father was struggling to untie, with nearly white fingers, his big black workboots. Lifting the latch, she was almost knocked over by the snowy gale that threw the door back.

"It's four, Mam, only four feet. I knew so. He'd four when Daddy went to town, and still four now."

"You little nanna," said my mam. "Close that door. We're not heating the yard."

"Did you get it, Dad?" I whispered, my back to my mother.

"I did. I've put it in an apple crate in the shed."

"What is it? Just whisper. I won't tell the others, promise."

"Now, would that be fair? You wait till Christmas morning, my love, the surprise will be yours, as well as your mam's."

"But Dad..."

"No buts. Scamper. Set up the table for supper."

This time of year was nearly unbearable. My stomach in a knot of anticipation from the end of November till The Great Day arrived. With nine children stretched across fifteen years, on a tiny mixed farm, Christmas always came with a share of anxiety. We couldn't help but hear Mam and Dad late at night—how were things, really? Could we afford a real Christmas this year? And what would it be like without Grammy, who'd gone from Antigonish County to her own ailing mam—so far away, all the way back to Ontario. And the biggest anxiety of all: could I find a Christmas present that would be good enough for the likes of my beautiful, hardworking, look-for-a-laugh-wherever-there-might-be-one, Mam, who gave a smile when you knew you should be in for a smack.

That's how she managed us. Folks now won't believe I grew up in a house where a voice was never raised to any of the nine, but it's true. I don't know to this day what the code was that flew between her and my father, but it kept them knowing each other's mind like some kind of magic.

We children divided into four groups: The two oldest boys, Barton and Ronald (the Big Boys), the two oldest girls, Meg and Alice (the Big Girls), the next three girls, Sheila, Sarah, and Sylvie (the Three S's), and last of all, Marta and me. The Tiny Two, mostly the Tinies, occasionally the Terrible Two, shortened too often to the Terribles.

In years past, my brothers and sisters would organize their Christmas gifts months in advance—planning, making, and only very occasionally buying, exactly the right thing. Such a lot of fun was in this, and every year the "natural order" of the family reasserted itself around the ritual of the gift giving.

Instead of trying to stretch our limited resources for Mam and Dad, we'd settled on the four-way split—a gift from each group—always with a certain amount of good-natured rivalry. Who had the funniest, cleverest, most useful, and for Mam, the most beautiful, gift. This year, though, Marta and I knew our gift would be the favoured one.

Helping her make our weekly batch of bread, miles from the Christmas season, I'd heard Mam say, "Oh, I wish I had some decent bowls!" And there it was. The perfect, wanted, useful thing. A beautiful bowl for the baking of bread.

So, Marta and I saved. We'd a hen each, and that fall sold our eggs to our teacher, having acquired exclusive rights to fill all her egg requirements. We put our pennies in an old sock under our shared bed. As Christmas crept closer, absolutely determined that our present would be a complete surprise, we negotiated with a neighbour to purchase the coveted object.

It lay, tightly wrapped and tied with string, potato-stamp stars scattered over the brown paper, under our bed, waiting. Loaves of bread for the family, and the beatific smile sure to be on Mam's face as she unwrapped it, were biding time with the beautiful bowl under hand-me-downs for the Tiny Two from the Big Girls.

Dad's arrival home from town that day, with his very own secret present for Mam—and those brown bags that must surely contain the Christmas oranges and the hard ribbon candy—marked the real beginning of the crazy sleigh-ride down the wintry hill towards Christmas. The school concert was that night, a pot-luck cèilidh with neighbours was planned for the next, a church social on Christmas Eve, and finally, creeping downstairs in the quiet house, to put our precious gift with a little pile of others. We stood, overwhelmed by the magic of a tree lit by moonlight in our small front room, then raced up to bed, as quiet as two Littles could who were full to the brim of excitement for...

The Day

At last. The frozen, snow-bright Christmas morning.

We wake to the clatter of coffee-making in the kitchen, the fire being laid. The moon not ready to set yet and the sun only thinking about lifting its lazy, watery face out of the Straight. The same wicked wind tipping the waves with white ice rushes, an eddy of snow to hide the shed not thirty feet from the house. It disappears and reappears like—my father! A now-you-see-him-now-you-don't figure carrying a parcel: his secret Christmas present for Mam.

Settling around the tree with coffee for Mam and Dad and all of us kids clutching mugs of the first-of-the-season hot milky chocolate, the ritual begins. As The Tinies, our gift gets first attention. The potato-stamp stars are exclaimed over; the skill of the careful folds praised as Mam unwraps far too slowly, saving the paper. But then, the rapture. Kisses and ecstasy for Marta and me. It is, says Mam, the perfect, the most useful, the most beautiful stainless steel bread bowl of gifts. She pulls us close, while across the room, *looks* exchanging, unnoticed by the Tinies in our joy.

Next for Mam, from the Three S's. Rustling through tissue paper, cadged from the schoolteacher, nestling sweetly one inside the next: a set of three bright red, perfectly beautiful, useful...bowls.

Joy from Mam, and a laugh and...looks exchanging.

Next, from the Big Girls. Cleverly wrapped in the funny papers this time. Li'l Abner and Daisy Mae fighting from strip to strip in black and white over what Mam begins to chuckle at before she's got it unwrapped.

"How many times did I say it?" she laughs, holding out the blue and white bowl, fragile and pretty but also practical with its lid. "Perfect," she says, "for potatoes."

The looks now just between the boys and Dad. And as she pulls apart the Big Boys' package, the tears start down her face as Mam's laughing catches her breath and makes her hiccup. This time, four. The biggest has a spout like a jug, with measurements marked on the side, and three more inside. Sturdy, self-satisfied, modern white...bowls.

"Perfect," says Mam, "for baking!"

"But not bread," say The Tinies.

"Everything but!" she agrees.

"And now," says Dad, "for mine."

With a shake to his voice, he carefully hands over his gift.

And it is...a bowl. A lovely glass bowl, clear right through, with a rose etched on each side.

My mother laughs and laughs and cries and cries and all of us do too.

"Did ever any woman have a listening-er family than mine? And look at the number. You got it just right. Ten. Ten bowls..."

"...and nothing else! Poor Mam!" a chorus from the Littles.

"Poor Mam? Oh no!" she says. "I've something else," she adds as she looks around at all of us, beaming, with tears still rolling down her face. "Something rare indeed."

A Goat's Christmas Carol

We three stood at the base of the street light, looking towards the neat, beige bungalow with Christmas lights draping the porch. Through the steam-frosted glass, the tree in the front window shimmered red, white, and green. We were frozen: by the wind whipping the freshly fallen snow, and with indecision.

"I don't know. We don't want to..."

My voice fell away. We don't want to...what? Make them sad? Make them happy? Make them remember and long for what might have been? All of us stood, thinking the same thoughts, pulled towards the little house, but caught in our own memories of the Christmas Eve before.

Exactly a year ago, we'd stood at the foot of this lamppost, and it had been snowing and cold—colder in fact—and we'd been four, like tonight. Filipe and James, myself, and Bianca, Filipe's beloved little goat.

That night Filipe had said, "Time to go home. It's 10:30. And it's snowing. And look, she's shivering."

"She trembles," said James. "Come on, Filipe. It's a goat thing. When she's not eating, she's trembling."

"I don't think I can accept that blatant prejudice; that's clear goatism."

A push, a snowbank, some rolling, some rubbing of faces with the fresh and still-falling snow. And then stillness. The four of us, including Bianca, lay on the dry white blanket and looked up into the Christmas Eve sky, stars shining with a more spectacular, more piercing brightness than usual. The Milky Way more path-like; Orion a braver, more daring sky hunter than even a week before.

"What is it, do you think? That makes a Christmas sky so magic?" I rolled over to face my friends.

"The goat, of course." From Filipe.

"Stop it. I mean it."

"So do I. The *goat*ential for great happenings."

I rubbed Bianca's muzzle. "She is special."

"Of course she is." From James.

"She's a bringer of joy." From Filipe, her besotted guardian.

Filipe and James, best friends to each other and to me, had convinced me that our search for the meaning of Christmas would only be successful if we found a way to give maximum joy to the maximum number of people in our village that Christmas Eve. And to Filipe, that meant sharing his love of singing and the sweetness of Bianca. So, we'd tied a red ribbon with a bell around the little goat's neck and coaxed her through the snow, door to door, then through the hallways of the town's tiny nursing home, singing and laughing with the old folks at Bianca's uninhibited shows of affection—although the nibbling could just have been hunger—and now, nearly at the end of the village, we were back in the snow again, lying on the lawn of the bungalow.

Sitting up, Filipe drew in a long breath, inhaling the snow and the sharp night air, then started in his most beautiful tenor, "O Holy Night." And the church bells began to ring eleven.

"We should go." I was getting to my feet when a voice I didn't recognize said, "Please don't. Come inside and sing for us. I can't tell you what it would mean."

We all turned to the voice coming from the steps of the bungalow, where a young man stood, pulling a sweater around himself. "That was lovely. It's just what we need. Please, come in and let us give you a drink—hot chocolate? Scotch? in exchange for a song. That's usually the deal, isn't it?"

"Bianca too?" Filipe wouldn't stand for the exclusion of his pet.

"Bianca too," laughed the young man. "We won't be accused of goatism here."

How long, I wondered, had he been there? Smiles of recognition all around as we trooped into the house, slipping off boots and unzipping on our way. In a small town you may not *know* everyone, but you've seen them, sometime. I knew the young man's face, and I definitely remembered seeing the lovely young woman, who sat in an ancient armchair in front of the blazing wood stove, cuddling a child wrapped chin to toes in a soft pale blanket.

"This is Maddie," said our host, "and her mum, Alison. And I'm Paul. Maddie, look at our visitors! What a treat! Singers and a lovely little kid."

The little girl sat up and examined us, then spoke with a kind of care and precision I'd never seen in a child.

"She's not a kid," said Maddie, "She's a goat. Are goats allowed in the house?"

"They are tonight," said her mother.

"Everything's different tonight, isn't it?" said Maddie.

"It is," said her father, with a sadness that was undeniable. He beckoned me into the small kitchen to get our drinks.

"Maddie's ill," he said. "Very ill. So, everything is different for us now. Two weeks ago, we'd never have imagined this would be her last Christmas. But..." He paused. "It's very aggressive. They don't expect more than a few weeks, if we're lucky. So." He shrugged, both hands open. "Everything is different."

I looked with a kind of shame at the generous glasses of whisky Paul had poured for us. Too large. Too celebratory. But we carried them back to the fire, where Filipe and James had begun "Away in a Manger" in close harmony, with Bianca the very picture of beatific beasthood. She'd knelt beside the chair where Alison and Maddie sat, and as I watched, Maddie slipped from her mother's lap to the floor, to look directly into Bianca's face as she stroked the goat's head. Bianca turned to her, those beautiful golden eyes with their strange horizontal pupils fixed on Maddie, unblinking. Watching as my friends made the inevitable small-town connections with our hosts between songs, I saw too, the bond growing between the child and goat as they bumped and nuzzled. The minutes flew past, and suddenly it was midnight and the bells from the churches began their cacophony, the Bapists, the Anglicans, and the Catholics all welcoming Christmas Day.

At quarter past when we rose—a little unsteadily, it must be said, having put away a considerable amount of Scotch between us—the little girl was curled beside the goat, Bianca's nose tucked firmly in Maddie's ear.

Alison untangled her sleeping child from the drowsy kid and lifted her to her shoulder, seeing us to the door.

"Thank you for this," she said, "It was pure magic."

"Christmas magic," murmured Maddie, not lifting her head, eyes closed. "Bye, Bianca. See you soon." And the goat, we all remembered, looked directly at Maddie, and with a final toss of her sweet goat head, bleated goodbye.

Her parents looked sadder than I imagined two lovely young people could look, standing on the porch with their slip of a daughter wrapped tightly in the blanket, waving us off into the snow.

I thought about Maddie often that year. I thought I saw her in the street, I thought I saw her parents. I should have seen them in such a small town. But I was never sure it was them, and I couldn't bear to ask someone who might have known.

But Christmas Eve had come again, and Filipe and James and my new husband and I had gone carolling again, sans Bianca, who'd gone to live with another goat friend when Filipe and James had to leave the little farm they'd been renting. Both losses that Filipe felt keenly. And now we'd arrived at the bungalow where we'd been so warmly welcomed the year before, and we stood in the cold, debating.

"I don't think I can bear it," I said, nursing my own new, sweet hope. "I don't think I can see their sad faces."

"We may be exactly what they need," said Filipe. "We'll know. If we're not, we'll leave."

So up the steps we went, and began a spirited version of "God Rest Ye Merry, Gentlemen." At once, the door was flung open by a child who seemed a *version* of Maddie but pinker, rounder, bolder, and brighter. And behind her, Alison. Calm and happy: a woman no longer transparent with grief.

"Come in, come in! We wondered if we'd see you again! We hoped you'd come—where's Bianca?" Paul had joined, and was urging us in.

We settled into the same warm room, with the same glowing wood stove, but there was definitely a new story woven around the little family. Paul and I went to the kitchen where out came the Scotch, and while he made the hot chocolate I was having instead, I tried to ask, delicately, but Paul would only say in answer to my question, "Ask Maddie."

So we did.

And Maddie told us. That when the bells had rung at midnight the Christmas Eve past, ushering in the miracle of Christmas Day, what Filipe had thought was Bianca's insatiable appetite for salty ears was, in fact, a present.

"A present?" I said to Maddie. "What sort of present?"

"A lovely one. A *one-word* one. A Christmas Eve, *once-only-ever* one."

"Ah." We visitors sent indulgent looks from one to another, to another. This charming child. "What word?" I asked.

Maddie turned to her mother who knew the story and knew the ending, and who nodded to her daughter with a sweetness that made my full heart ache. The sweet pain of my own hopes sharing that crowded space with Alison's too. And Maddie said,

"*Live.*"

Reaching for her mother's hand and looking at her father, whose eyes were full.

"She said, live."

A Wheel of Cheese

In her dream, her mother was dancing. She knew the woman was her mother because she wore one of her mother's beautiful dancing dresses, Ally's favourite of all the dresses, something swishy and green—the exact colour of pine buds in the spring—with feathers ringing the hem. Feathers called—oh she knew, she knew the name, her mother had told her, she just couldn't...they came from storks. The birds that brought babies. Though Ally knew they didn't *actually* bring babies, but people still said they did. Brought them and left them in cabbage patches. Why cabbage? Why not rose gardens? Oh, thorns of course, thought Ally in her dream.

What they should be saying, she thought, was that they came and dropped their magical feathers for people like her mother to sew into long dangly scarves; for women with bright red lips and dark eyes to throw round their shoulders while they lit cigarettes in long holders—not her mother though, she would *never* smoke—or, to stitch onto the bottom of dresses that billowed. That made the dress behave like a fuzzy, living hula hoop.

Like her mother's dress, moving round her mother's knees as she twirled and laughed in the living room, trying out the dress before she wore it, before Ally's mom *went out* for the very first time Ally could remember. To a dance. With other grown-ups, including boys—well, men—who Ally and her mother didn't know. The Minus One Club, her mother said, a name that really bothered Ally. Even in the dream, she felt a niggle knowing where her mother was going.

So yes. It was definitely her mother in her dream, her in the green dress. But instead of the round face framed with reddish-blond curls she knew, this version of her mother had a delicate pointy nose, two sweet pink ears with tiny white tufts, and sneaking out from beneath the—wait, marabou!—around the hem, a pale grey tail waved, tied at the end with a tiny matching green ribbon. Around the mouse's plump shoulders floated a delicate boa of the same wispy stuff. Marabou. That was name of the fancy feathery trim.

Dreams were such peculiar places. Ally watched her mother from a distance that kept shifting from very close-up, close enough to count the tiny hairs in the tufts of her mother's ears, to far away, across a vast room. Like looking through the wrong end of a stethoscope. No. Hmm. Telescope? And then the perspective would change again and she'd be peering down, as if she were flying. So high above that her mother was only a speck, but Ally still could make out every detail as she watched the beautifully dressed mouse lady, her mother, climb up into a carriage just like Cinderella would have climbed into that pumpkin, helped by a handsome mouse-man with a large, curly-twirly moustache and white wavy hair.

This carriage didn't look at all like a pumpkin though, and the thing that made it especially different from Cinderella's was that the wheels were enormous, round wheels of cheese. Gouda. Ally knew for absolutely sure they were Gouda from the printing on each wheel. And she knew what Gouda was and where it came from, because last night a white-haired man had knocked at their front door and her mother had let him in, turning pink right to the tips of her ears, smiling in a way Ally had not seen her smile in...well, ever. She'd never seen her mother smile like that.

White-haired. That makes him sound old, Ally had thought, waking and rolling over to see her mom leaning against her doorframe. But he's not. He's just... like an elf.

Breakfast? her mom asked.

Mm maybe not yet?

Mm maybe you'll miss the school bus?

Mm maybe it's a snow day.

Her mom turned with a laugh. Mm maybe not. Open your curtains, it's pouring sun out.

Ally had crawled from her bed, yanking the curtains to see white-silver-gold-white, a rolling paragraph of winter, punctuated by the tiny pine trees her mom had planted when they moved in last year. Already settled and bigger. She and her mother had walked by the train tracks, her mom with a little shovel and burlap bag, digging up the "babies, who just want their very own place to thrive." Her mom knew.

Ally's brother had told her their mom left home twice: once when she ran away to be with their dad, and once when she ran away from him.

Don't don't don't, Ally thought. The sun is shining, don't think of Dad. He's okay. He's better now. There's a Chinook coming. Oh no. Don't melt the snow for Christmas. Please let there be snow for—

Ally!

Coming!

She stretched for the carefully laid out clothes on her chair, doing her trick: one pyjama leg off at a time for warmth, then one leg of her undies, then her jeans, then the other leg, same process.

Ally!

It took a minute, this process.

Her mom went to school now too. She taught in the high school, so when Ally got home, she wasn't always there. Aggie was. Ally loved Aggie. She had white hair and wore an apron—her pinnie, she called it—and she *was* old. Not just the sort of white-hair old of the Elf Man. Aggie told Ally that she was quite close to a hundred, but was a medical miracle: she'd had so many operations she'd been "written up." Whatever that meant.

Today Ally stepped into the fragrant kitchen all spice and sweet with baking and Aggie's own particular scent, and continued to peel off the layers required for the four-block walk on a minus-plus day. That's what Ally's mom called it. They didn't bother with actual numbers. It was either minus-minus or minus-plus and when it was minus-minus, you had four or five layers, and if it was minus-plus, like it was today because of the Chinook, you only had two or three.

Ally hugged Aggie, smiled, and politely answered all the requisites—Good day? Got homework? Where's yer brother? Gonna do some piany?—as she waited for the tray of cookies Aggie pulled from the oven to land on the counter.

Yup, said Ally. Yup. He's at basketball. Yup.

Yer ma having a big Christmas party!

What? Is she?

No. Li'l girl, it's a question. Is yer ma having a party? She's got a huge wheel of cheese in the cold room.

Oh. I know. No, I don't think. Well, maybe. Maybe she is. But the cheese was a present.

A present? Good lord, who gives that much cheese.

I know. I dunno. A sort of Elf Man guy.

A what?

A kind of...he's not very tall and he's sort of strong looking, with wavy white hair and sparkly eyes and—

Santa!?

Ally studied Aggie. Did she still believe in Santa? Better be careful, just in case.

No. Don't think so. No. Skinny-strong. Just a...Mom met him. At that dance. Remember? The Minus—

Oh, I do.

Aggie pursed her mouth in her funny way, like she wanted to smile but just wouldn't.

Yeah. A while ago. He came to visit. She didn't say?

No she didn't. Huh.

And Aggie stood looking out at the Chinook arch, with a very slow smile growing. Ally loved when Aggie grew a smile. It didn't happen often.

You look glad, Ally said, and she reached for a cookie, still hot. Do you like cheese?

And then Aggie laughed. Ally couldn't remember hearing her laugh that long before. Aggie laughed and she kept laughing as she turned away from the Chinook. She laughed when she said, I love cheese. Cheese straws, cheese sauce, cheese sandwiches, cauliflower cheese with bacon, cheese with apple pie. And I bet yer ma will love all those things too. And more.

Then Aggie was done laughing. So, she said, looking hard at Ally, you met him. Did you like him?

Ally considered. Was this a trick question? What would her brother say? What did her brother think?! She wasn't sure, as Andrew had gone very quiet since the Elf Man brought the cheese. She knew the top layer of Aggie's question was only that: the top layer. Aggie was asking a whole bunch of other things too. About her mom, about Ally and Andrew. About their dad. About change and being afraid and going forward with tiny little shuffles, decisions that wouldn't take anyone to the edge of any kind of canyon.

Ally viewed decisions as steps toward a gorge where, at the bottom there might be a beautiful, warm, slow-flowing river, or a massive pillow of marshmallow or feathers, or, just as possible, a deep crevasse of anger and fear and blackness and yelling. She didn't want any more yelling. Or hurting, for her mom. Or her brother. Or, an afterthought, for herself.

Ally always stood a very long time on the edge of that canyon.

And what she'd felt when the Elf Man walked through the door with his wheel of cheese was what she'd *decided* to feel, as she watched her mother laugh, surprised and so happy with the gift of cheese this close to Christmas. She liked the careful way he'd come through the door into their home. Not reaching for the handle himself but knocking, then waiting outside on the cold step for Ally to open it and not stepping inside until her mom had said, Well hello! And what on earth are you carrying, come in, come in! She liked the quiet way he'd come inside, smiling at her mom while carefully setting the wheel of cheese down, and then, staying down, kneeling eye to eye with her, and saying, You must be Ally. You won't believe all the good things I've heard about you.

And then he put his elf-hand out for her to shake and no one ever, ever before, had looked to shake Ally's hand. She liked him not smelling of cigarettes, or of anything but soap and water.

So she shook his hand, smiling, and he stood up again, and her mother kissed his cheek. Ally stared. Her mother had only ever kissed her and her brother.

And her dad, she remembered. Once. Oh don't don't don't. Aggie was looking at her.

That's a long think, she said.

I know, said Ally. There's a lot to think about.

There always is with you, missy. Have another cookie?

Ally took another, the chocolate chips still hot and runny.

Every day when Ally came home and Aggie handed her a cookie and said, you okay missy, Aggie knew that fresh cookie was a story neither of them had to talk about. Aggie told it handing Ally the cookie and Ally answered by eating the cookie and saying, that was the best cookie ever in the world. And Aggie always said, I know that little missy. Because it's for you.

Ally licked all around her mouth, and turned to Aggie.

I do like him.

Aggie smiled in her non-smiley way at Ally, wiped her hands on her apron, and turned off the oven.

Maybe, said Aggie, as she squirted the dish soap (*tough on grease, soft on hands*) I'll make yer ma some cheese straws tomorrow.

She'll like that, said Ally. Should I dry for you?

You do that, little missy.

Ally took the dishtowel, and Aggie started a little hum as they tidied up the dishes.

Angel in Tompkins Square

On this blindingly sunny Christmas Day, on a bench in New York City, Kate sat next to a stranger. A woman in an ankle-length fur coat whose nails were surely too long for her to blow her own nose—and how could she possibly do dishes? Fold laundry?

Fur Coat Woman shaded her eyes against the sun and gestured to a huge elm tree, where a crowd had gathered. "The squirrel's going to be Christmas dinner if he's not careful," she said, pointing to the imposing hawk that had been thrilling visitors to the park for the last week, sailing silently overhead, then finally, yesterday, striking. "That thing took a dog yesterday—one of those toy types. Swooped and scooped." She laughed a little, then shook her head, admonishing herself. "It's not funny. Poor little thing."

Kate winced, watching, remembering. Only the hawk's head moved as it followed every leap of the chattering, teasing squirrel, who danced from one branch to the next, at the top of the elm tree.

Fur Coat Woman continued: "That dog was her baby. Just turned her back and—whoosh. She came back last night and found the coat, a little pink coat with toggles. You know, like on a duffel coat? She loved those toggles. The owner, I mean, not the dog. They only came on Sundays—apparently, it's a better crowd on Sundays. You'd have thought this was a Mensa dog the way she talked. The owner, not the dog..."

Kate wasn't a city person; this trip had been her daughter Christina's suggestion. Christina's idea for Kate to stay in a stranger's home in this overwhelming metropolis, to fumble her way through the labyrinthine subway system, shop in overpriced stores, and sit at tables-for-one in restaurants serving enormous portions.

Christina had been quick to organize her mother for the holidays when it became clear that some change to the usual family Christmas was inevitable. She claimed this was the time for Kate to be independent and curious and daring. That stung.

Kate thought she *was* independent and curious and daring. She also knew that she was fragile and needy and angry, and none of those were an easy sell for a Christmas houseguest.

So Christina found her mother a tiny, central Manhattan sublet on Craigslist. The flat's resident, a buxom, bespectacled NYU professor, met Kate at the door, introduced her to the grossly overweight cat now in Kate's care, handed over her keys and emergency contacts, then rushed for a flight to meet her Italian lover in Rome. Kate watched her from three floors up, pulling her designer suitcase toward the subway in her absurdly high heels, until she disappeared. When Kate turned, the fat cat was clawing an ancient sofa and glaring at her. She wanted to leave.

But of course she didn't. She needed to be getting out of herself—well, away from herself. Leaving her small, chatty town. Challenging herself in all kinds of new ways, but most notably she thought, putting aside her prejudices toward Americans. At first, Kate felt magnanimous as she gently excused these people the accident of their birth and government. Gradually though, she realized she was genuinely enjoying the differences she itemized daily.

Volume. Energy. Intensity. Independence. Curiosity. Daring. She revelled in the outfits, the costume on the streets, and surprisingly, in the interest New Yorkers seemed to take in her every time she pulled out her map book. Pulling the map book out seemed to magically produce a couple of strangers ready to offer unsolicited advice. So odd. The way New Yorkers were prepared to participate in other people's lives confounded her expectations. Or perhaps it was just *her* life. It was...definitely not Canadian.

She was delighted by the Broadway audience who exploded with laughter three lines into the preview of a new political play. "Why do they hate me?" the actor playing the president whined. "Well, sir," said his advisor, "because you've fucked the country." While Kate didn't care for the character's vocabulary, the sentiment accelerated her nascent generosity and growing fondness for her North American neighbours. For this fur-clad woman, sitting beside her now. Kate studied her from behind dark glasses, admired the complexity of her carefully coloured and styled hair, her full lips the exact colour of those nails, and the long, long eyelashes that were lifted, like Kate's now, to the treetop. Kate watched the hawk, but saw the eagle.

When Christina left for university and Marc took early retirement, Kate had told her determinedly urban husband that it was her turn to choose. Throughout their marriage, Marc chose their houses for utility and thrift, for proximity to his workplaces and Christina's schools. But this time, Kate had insisted on this decaying cottage on two acres in the Valley with no proximity to anything. Her first house choice was just down the road from Paradise, Nova Scotia. The most fertile and beautiful part of the province, much of which was gradually being turned into vineyards: *the new Provence*, locals claimed.

Kate loved it. A Buddhist friend said her home had perfect feng shui, situated for success and comfort and joy and balance. Kate quickly assumed a spiritual connection to the land, guarded, she felt, by the eagles—she'd counted eight one day—that perched in the majestic pines on the edge of the property. Her connections on the property weren't limited to the animate: she'd developed—a result, she thought of underutilized maternal instincts—a curious sympathy for the tipsy outbuildings and the ancient septic system. She knew the system was fragile, though she'd never had a septic system before and didn't fully grasp wherein that fragility lay, but as recommended by a back-to-the-land-friend she'd made in the natural food store, she fed the septic active dry yeast, and she got their carpenter husband—she was Mary and he was Joseph; that seemed auspicious—to come prop up the listing outbuildings.

Kate designed and micromanaged every inch of their extensive renovation and was thrilled with her achievements. Every vista, framed by every window and changed by every season, delighted her, but especially the magnificent sweep of the huge furrowed hill at the back. It went from grey, to limey new-green, to emerald, then gold, then silver-white. She learned to love winter there, snowshoeing for the first time along the edge where the forest met the winter-suede field.

Every penny they had (and many they didn't, Marc said—often) financed the renovation. Kate's days were filled with colours, light fixtures, fabrics. Just this way and not that. One decision forcing another. Kate was irritated by Marc's repeated *When are we done?* but resented the implied question even more. She didn't feel she was proving anything to anyone. She built a deck, changed the windows, added a skylight over the narrow staircase. She wouldn't settle until every corner was re-created, a testament to her commitment to homey, aesthetic perfection. She imagined herself a kind of alchemist, turning the leaden length of winter into squares of gold: light pouring through the expensive windows and skylights, falling onto polished wooden floors and stairs. The house, her house, was a story; a poem crafted from wood and glass and fabric; a painting of gracious domesticity framed by the river and the hill. The eagles high above the skylight—loops and ovals and tight, perfect circles—were the signature on her work of art.

And on the edge of the canvas, the animals.

First: a pair of tiny, flea-infested kittens dumped on their drive Halloween night. Wicked. They'd never had pets; Marc didn't like animals indoors. Promising to take the kittens to the vet, Kate fed them—just till they got their strength up—in the tipsy shed. She took them bowls of milk and kitten mush for nearly two weeks, and then, with the first snowfall, they moved indoors. She put a card on the bulletin board in the convenience store, written lightly in pencil, offering them up, and thumbtacked it to the bottom of the board. No one claimed them, poor things. Cats made a home. Two cats in the yard.

And really, in the country, a dog was better than the burglar alarm that Marc wanted. So, one February day, she dragged her reluctant husband to an animal shelter at the end of the province, just exploring the possibility of adopting a puppy she'd seen online. Two hundred winter miles was a long drive for an exploration. The puppy came home...and got violently ill. The vet's bills were twice as much as the cost of any bespoke dog that might have been delivered to their door from a reputable kennel, as Marc became very fond of pointing out. The puppy spent days on intravenous at the vet, Kate holding it in her arms. What, Marc asked, did Kate think she might renovate next?

He didn't touch the dog, or the cats. He spent hours in his study, quiet melodies from Radio Two slipping underneath his closed door like furtive cigarette smoke, wraiths hugging the floor. Kate didn't like classical music. That was why he closed his door, she supposed.

Several times a night Kate was up and down to the frozen garden, carrying the sickly puppy, who was terrified of the narrow staircase—and the cats who slept one step from the top, always malicious, or playful, but certainly dangerous, obstacles to what was inevitably an urgent descent—tightly in her arms. Set safely at the bottom, the puppy still couldn't make it to the back door without leaving a foul-smelling trail to be cleaned up at three in the morning.

When Christina had been born, Marc would get up in the night to warm a hot water bottle for their daughter's crib while Kate nursed, binding them in a midnight contract which they'd carried like something precious through their days. This nocturnal companionship did not re-emerge with the puppy. Marc rolled over at first whimper, pulled the pillow around his head, and lay very, very still.

Eventually the dog got well, and got big. A piece of moving furniture, Marc said. The dog learned to love the cats and played with the smallest, the calico, dragging it around ever so gently with its head in his mouth. Marc found this disconcerting. Irritating. Kate thought it sweet and funny that the tiny calico, a perpetual kitten, would extract her head from the dog's jaws looking like a bemused punk rocker—hair at all angles and a slightly stoned look—regaining her cat composure with a shake of her head. Then she'd go back, purring and weaving in and out of the dog's legs, while the other cat hid. Kate knew that, just as a parent shouldn't love one child more than another, a pet owner shouldn't have favourites. But she couldn't help it. She loved that calico for the fleas it had overcome, and the tolerance it displayed now for the dog.

There were other creatures, too. Deer in the garden. Racoons tipping the garbage. Skunks that sprayed the tires of the car, God knows why. Because they could, Marc said. Revenge for roadkill relatives. And porcupines, one of whom became intimately acquainted with the dog. Or rather, the dog with him. Or her. Hard to tell with a porcupine, thought Kate. And hard to define that discomfiting combination of embrace and attack. Which was what her marriage was beginning to feel like. Embrace, though, was...infrequent.

But the kicker, as her daughter would say, Kate thought, watching the New York hawk step delicately towards the teasing squirrel, the kicker was the eagle.

This park had loomed large in one of Christina's favourite films, according to the notes she'd emailed her mother urging her to do a movie tour of the city. That musical, *RENT*, featuring Tompkins Square as the haunt of squatters and the homeless, had made Kate cringe. An ode to junkies, she thought. To what passed for love, in the age of AIDS. To rock and roll—which was exhausting, Kate thought, never really a music fan; to the forced responsibility for friends who became family and strangers who become intimates. It all made her shudder. But, Christina said, it represented comfort in a world of urban distance and alienation.

Now, though, the park had been cleaned up, renovated, and was a kind of bucolic oasis. A city idyll for the city idle. A place of elms: a genus of tree virtually wiped out in Kate's valley by Dutch elm disease but thriving here, and in fact, Fur Coat Woman reported, holy.

"Under that tree," she explained, "a Hare Krishna Swami held the first open-air chanting of their sacred mantra outside India. Allen Ginsberg, you know the *Howl* guy? He was here. Sort of after, no, maybe during the Vietnam stuff. Before the druggie stuff. I was here for all that." She sighed, reminiscing. "My neighbour—not the dog one, another one—was filming the riot from his stoop and the police came over and beat him up."

How many of those gathered around the tree now, Kate wondered, had come here this Christmas Day to remember a friend lost to riot, to drugs, to loneliness? Perhaps, like her, they'd only come to sit in the unseasonably warm sunshine, avoiding a Christmas table set for one, and, like her, had been captivated by this incursion of wildlife into their cityscape. This new danger in their park.

The hawk dropped down a branch. Kate squinted against the sun.

It was September and midday hot with the ferocity of finality. Every window in the house was opened to tempt breezes to cross the too-still rooms. Kate had come onto the deck with her lunch and several decorating magazines. The dog lay panting by her side, shifting every so often to stay in the shadow she cast. The tiny calico cat dozed beside the rain barrel that sat away from them, against the house, casting the only small triangle of shade in the open backyard. A hundred yards away the trees were a black fringe on the green corduroy hill, the long bolt of farmland running from the house up to the horizon.

Suddenly a shriek from the nearest pine cut the custard-like air of the afternoon. The dog started from his doze; the cat stirred, springing lightly to the edge of the deck. She sat licking one paw, squinting into the bright distance, then peering at the other paw, moggy-myopic.

And then, a sound Kate would never forget. A shivering, or shuddering, of wings. Enormous wings against resistant air. Angels? She smiled at her own fancy, standing and shading her eyes against the sun. Another shriek, closer now. Not benign, haloed visitors then. Dragons? Still smiling, she brushed back the hair that blew across her face as a terrible cry from the calico cat rent the still afternoon.

Kate's breath deserted her, pulled away by the force of those wings, so close, leaving her dizzy. She was rooted, grasping to understand the moment, until a cruel, triumphant bawl from the massive bird set her running, barefoot and stumbling, to the base of the hill. She chased her thrashing pet, held fast in the talons of the eagle flying almost lazily just above the furrowed rising slope, the kitten's feet nearly dragging at first, then up and up. Wings out, wings in; higher and higher, and finally eclipsing, for a moment, the sun.

Kate began to shake, suddenly cold. The dog whined next to her, transfixed too, as the winged beast swept up the side of the beautiful green bowl of the valley, creating eddies in the dust between the crop rows as it dwindled into the distance, and then vanished over the top.

Marc came at her screams and said, "What on earth is it?"

"My cat. My cat," she wept. "An eagle has taken my cat."

Marc looked up the hill, then walked back inside.

Kate travelled by train from Montreal to New York, stopping over briefly in Boston, and walking around the Common. Artists were working on ice sculptures all over the park and the largest was an enormous, transparent eagle. She stood rigid in the cold. Frightened and alone, staring at a monster.

She'd been anxious about filling the days before Christmas, but once settled in Manhattan, every day, as if it was her job, she took Christina's film notes, stuck her map book in her pocket, and went searching. She made her way to Tiffany's, knowing better than to expect breakfast; to Macy's to see the windows, the Christmas marketing miracle of 34th Street; and to the

Chrysler Building, glinting in the December sunlight like an exquisite piece of Art Deco jewelry the wrong way up. I'd wear that, Kate thought, if it were jet and silver.

On every expedition, Kate was guided by curious and opinionated New Yorkers. She was informed, educated, even teased. The diner from *When Harry Met Sally...* was her favourite. She had a Rueben and a moment. Remembering the old-world courtesy of the silver-haired, wire-rimmed-glasses man who flirted so delicately made her smile.

Arriving at the last of the locations on Christina's tour, the Life Café near Tompkins Square, Kate had been quizzed by the bartender and found herself telling him, rather shamefacedly, what she'd been doing. Sweet young man, he didn't think she was a gawker of celebrity haunts. He applauded her strategy, loved her diverse list of films. She didn't tell him they were Christina's choices. He loved *RENT*, was proud of it. "Here," he said, "sit here." Jonathan had sat where he settled her, getting through endless cups of coffee and writing his play. So Kate had stayed and stayed, drunk coffee, then eaten, then had a glass of wine, then another coffee, and talked as she hadn't talked for years to the young bartender who'd known Jonathan, and missed him. She wondered if she'd missed something, something important, in *RENT*, and resolved to watch it again. Perhaps with Christina. Kate discovered she missed her daughter as she hadn't in years, feeling closer to Christina than when they'd last been together, and her eyes misted over, understanding a little now the reverence for that young playwright gone too soon, too young.

Kate had followed Marc through the house, screaming and crying. She watched herself from a distance, astonished by the assault she turned on him. Nor did she recognize the white-hot fury that grew in him, or the words he found to express it. Months of near silence, conversations hewn from two or three words, necessities, gave way now to a frightening eloquence. Words describing his anger, his boredom. His loathing. And words she'd never imagined for lonely. Mine, she thought. Those are my words, not yours. Where had he found this fluency, absent in nearly thirty years of marriage? Perhaps, Kate had thought, pausing on the narrow stairs in a rectangle of sunlight after Marc had slammed the door, perhaps that was what he was doing in his study with the door closed. Reading the thesaurus.

A single unearthly shriek, and then, wails. Echoes of disbelief bouncing off Charlie Parker's brownstone and St. Brigid's Church.

Everyone was on their feet. The hawk had taken off and soared and circled, then suddenly, shockingly, dropped onto the squirrel, before rising again, winging towards the church, the squirrel flailing beneath him. The game was over.

Kate watched. Beside her, Fur Coat Woman watched too. They stood shoulder to shoulder, like members of a congregation, drawing deep, then ragged, breaths. Kate's eyes filled, and she wondered if her new friend was crying too.

Crying for the squirrel who thought the game was one thing, and not what it became; for Jonathan Larson, who never knew he won the Pulitzer Prize; for Christina and her unexpected burden; for Marc and his quiet radio; for the bruised faces and eyes and hearts of those who'd protested here, who'd wept or died for freedom under these majestic trees; for all the Christmas tables everywhere with one place setting; and for the calico kitten and the marriage taken over the sweep of the corduroy hill by a creature with wings that had sounded, Kate knew now, not like a dragon's at all.

The Compass

Juliette rubbed a little circle in the condensation of the bus window. Sarah was riding like a child on her tall boyfriend's shoulders, so her face was level with Juliette's; her friend was shouting and laughing, and waving.

"I can't hear you, Sarah. It's too noisy." More waving, louder shouting. "Sarah, you idiot. Aaron, let her down! Get on your bus, you two! You'll miss it! Git!"

Pressing her cheek against the cold window to mouth kisses to her friends on the forecourt of the bus depot, Juliette waved and waved as they backed off toward their own bus. She pulled her coat close and shifted her backpack into the seat next to her. Bus journeys made her territorial. She was determined not to get stuck next to some chatty church warden for the long trip home, so she'd spread out to inhabit both seats in her row. She hoped it looked like she was saving a place for someone.

Sarah's bus was pulling out now, but Juliette couldn't see anyone through the steamy windows. She rubbed her little circle clear again, only to have it filled in by thick clumps of snow limpets, clinging to each other in the rising wind. Why would anyone travel in the winter?

Christmas. A time when we're drawn back home whether we want to be or not. Like the arm of a compass swinging to North, we're pulled back to those who wait for us there...and those who don't.

The hairs on the back of Juliette's neck bristled. Someone was standing over the unoccupied seat next to her, willing her to turn around. She resisted but, aware of the door closing, looked towards the back of the bus and saw that nearly every seat was taken. She sighed as she moved her backpack, and a young woman swathed in a huge scarf covered with snow, bags in either hand, settled beside her. She must have been waiting outside for ages, Juliette thought. She looked frozen.

"Thanks. Sorry—don't mean to crowd you, but it's full up front, and I get sick when I sit in the back."

"Oh. Right." Juliette edged toward the window.

"I'm fine here, really. Relax. And I won't talk. I promise."

Juliette looked at the young woman, who, with her long dark hair and grey-green eyes, was so striking, and realized how rude she'd been.

"Sorry. I mean, it's okay. I'm just...tired. It's been a long trip."

"Oh, so you're not just starting here?"

"No. I'm at university in Toronto, coming home for Christmas, arriving in this." She gestured to the snowstorm raging beyond their window. "Our flight landed in Montreal 'cause they thought we couldn't land here, but then we took off again and got to Halifax hours late. Winter travel in Canada. I don't know why it always surprises everyone."

The bus started to manoeuvre its way through crawling rush-hour traffic and the driver picked up his microphone, announcing Sackville, Wolfville, and all stops through the Annapolis Valley to Yarmouth.

"Oh, man," said Juliette under her breath, "it's a slow one. Ah well."

The young woman beside her smiled. "Is there any other kind?"

"I guess not. At least we didn't get the Celtic Express."

"The Celtic Express?" the woman asked.

"One of the drivers loves fiddle music. Plays it from here to Yarmouth."

"That's a lot of fiddle music. Kind of unexpected."

Juliette raised an eyebrow. "You must be a come-from-away. I don't think I'd say fiddles are unexpected here. The weather now, that's unexpected. Or at least unpredictable. But even the unpredictable-ness becomes routine."

"I'm beginning to see that. And yes, I am a come-from-away. And I still love being snowed in..." She was unwinding her long, multicoloured scarf.

Juliette turned. "You *like* that?"

"Well, yes." The woman smiled. "I like the novelty of it. It's kind of romantic. Well, it has been so far. But then, we haven't been married long. And we've only been snowed in once. And it just doesn't happen where I come from. You know. Big-city girl getting back to the land... Sorry. I said I wouldn't talk."

"No, it's okay. I don't mind. Back to the land? Really?"

"Yes. I've been here about three months and this was my first trip into Halifax on my own!"

"On your own?" Juliette realized she must have sounded judgmental—the young woman was apologetic.

"Well, without my husband. Pathetic, isn't it? In this day and age? Not to be getting out and about more. But my baby's so interesting at the moment, I hate leaving her. I might miss something."

Juliette found herself charmed as the young woman described her life on a farm in the Valley not far, it seemed, from Juliette's home. The stop before her own. Her husband's family, she said, had been on the land for years but he'd only recently returned after a long time away and was trying now to turn it into an organic farm. He wasn't exactly, from what Juliette gathered, a natural farmer, but was so committed to learning it all yesterday, and spent so much time in his fields that, the young woman laughed, "I'm often afraid he's just lost his way home, he's always so late." She grinned. "You know men and directions."

The young woman pulled a little parcel out of her purse. "Can I show you this? I'm dying to show someone." She unwrapped a little bundle of tissue paper as Juliette watched, then held up something shining for her to see.

The watch glinted silver, catching light from the overhead pinpoint meant for reading and bouncing it in tiny slivers around them. The watch was unlike any

Juliette had seen; it had another, smaller face set just above the centre.

"It's a compass too," said the young woman. "So he can find his way back to me from the fields."

"It's beautiful." Juliette could not explain why her eyes were filling.

"Oh, and look." The woman dug into the voluminous bag again. "Listen, you really can tell me to be quiet, I don't mind..."

"No, it's fine. Honestly."

"Okay, this is the last thing. Things. You'll see." This time, she unwrapped a baby-sized pair of red leather shoes. Delicate little Mary Jane–style, with a wee sparkling button to fasten the strap.

"Oh, how sweet," breathed Juliette. "They are just..."

"Magic, aren't they? She'll take her first steps in these, I know she will. And red seemed to make a statement about where her shoes might take her eventually."

Juliette laughed. "You're right. I'm sure red shoes visit much more interesting places than your basic black."

And they both laughed at that, then settled into a companionable silence. Juliette turned away to stare into the storm, surprised to find tears welling again. What on earth was it about this young woman that made her feel so...raw?

There was something quite...quite *other* about her, thought Juliette. Beautiful, but more than that. She had a kind of fragility, and yet was so vibrant, so alive, that her nearly transparent skin seemed to glow. Her voice, as she spoke about her young family, was infused with colour and warmth, making everything she said compelling; it reached into Juliette, clutching her gut and twisting ever so gently.

Juliette had long been aware of other people's happy families: mothers besotted with their babies; parents still holding hands after twenty years—like Sarah's did. She was used to her own family, such as it was. Her dad, who worked dawn till dark on the farm where she'd grown up, and the succession of "ladies that do," as her dad had called the women who kept house for them. Women from her village who'd taken turns caring for Juliette in the early days after her mother left. Juliette had loved all of them, and they'd loved her; each woman giving her something different, like those good fairies in *Sleeping Beauty,* she thought. Each bestowing a gift, but not able to undo completely the harm done by the wicked fairy. But they hadn't, she thought, given anything much to her dad. Because her dad had decided he'd never look for anything from anyone again, apart from Juliette.

Juliette remembered the day—was she ten?—when her father had told her as much. She'd come home quiet and angry, determined not to let him see how upset she was. Determined he should know nothing about the bullying. She would not remind him of everything that had made him so quiet and self-contained, as Margie, their current "lady" had described him. Almost everything Juliette knew about why her father was the way he was had come from this series of well-meaning gossips. He just didn't talk much. Not about himself. He'd talk about the farm, about football and hockey and baseball; about her, and how proud he was of her, on every little occasion; but his own sadness or anger was kept well concealed. On this day though, having asked about school as they ate the meal that had been left for them, he looked up and watched her jaw working as she tried not to cry, saying the day had been fine.

"Funny fine that makes you cry," he'd said. "What happened?"

Juliette thought back now to the way he'd laid down his knife and fork and sat back in his chair with the question. There was nothing for it. He expected an answer and he expected the truth.

"Jason Burton said my mother ran away with a travelling salesman. He said she was an actress—like I didn't know that—and that all actresses are whores and that she couldn't be a whore in this town, so she left. And then Marney said she left because she didn't love us. Didn't love me."

"Marney your *friend*?" he'd asked. Juliette nodded, rubbing her eyes hard to stop the tears.

Dust drifted through the early evening sunlight that slanted through the kitchen blinds. The striped light across her father and the falling motes made her feel that his face was shifting, growing old, old, old as she looked at him. He closed his eyes.

"Your mother could pretend many things, Juliette, but she couldn't pretend it was easy for her here. I knew she missed her old life, but I thought she'd come to love this one. I thought she did love it. Love me. I don't think she *acted* her love for you. But...sometimes you can be wrong about people. You think you know their very centre, and yet..."

"Yet?" Juliette looked hard at her dad. His voice was ragged, and he wasn't looking at her now. He was staring through the window, she remembered, looking out to the pastures.

"Yet, you can't. You can never know someone else's heart. I understand that now. I don't know much, but I know that. I can't tell you what happened or why it happened or how, and I have to live every day with whatever my failure was. Except," and he looked at Juliette and smiled again, working at that smile, "it's not really a failure, because I have you."

They sat in silence. The dust kept falling, and her grandmother's old kitchen clock tick-ticked off the long moments as they sat, motionless, at the table. Their dinner was growing cold now.

"Where do you think she went, Dad?"

"I don't know, Jule."

"Don't you think she would at least be curious about me? That she'd want to know something about me?"

"I don't know, Jule. I've always hoped so. I keep hoping."

"Did you look really hard, Dad? Did you try really hard to find her?" Juliette was crying now, and when she looked back to her father she realized that he was too. Silently. Shockingly. Tears stalling in the late-day whiskers around his mouth. She'd never seen him cry. She'd never heard him speak of her mother, never heard him call her by name. He didn't name her now.

Frances. Frances who'd left when Juliette was just about to turn one. Gone the day before her birthday, Christmas Eve.

"I looked, and so did the police. We looked and looked. Everywhere. I still look. I think I see her sometimes." He was silent a moment and then, "I thought it might be easier to know something dreadful happened to her, something that would explain why she couldn't come back, rather than what everyone here believes—that she didn't want to come back."

"But Dad, she wouldn't—"

"—Jule. Let's stop." It was too much, Juliette realized now, though she hadn't then, to have his heart broken again. With rehashing, reimagining. "We're lucky. We've got each other. That's enough."

So they stopped, and that was all Juliette knew about her mother. Apart from what she'd heard people say in the hushed way they spoke of the dead, or the very wicked. She'd been lovely; she'd been funny;

she'd been wild and impulsive and stubborn; and she was clever, and kind and warm, Margie said. She made you look at things differently. She could talk you round to just about anything. Margie had loved her.

No pictures, no letters. Her father had kept nothing, purging his pain by burning everything Frances had left behind. That's what Margie had said. That he wouldn't even give her clothes away. Margie could understand that; he didn't want to see his wife's clothes walking toward him on Main Street. He made a big pile behind the barn and set it alight. He talked to no one for days and days. And then, the casseroles and freshly baked bread stopped appearing on the porch and the succession of ladies began. Juliette's good fairies.

Now, as the bus crawled further into the tunnel of snow, Juliette pressed her face hard against the cold window, drawn into the impenetrable whiteness. White darkness. It was late now; the city lights far behind, and nothing but the occasional headlights.

Every Christmas had been the same since Juliette had left for school. When she returned for the holidays, the closer she got to her stop, the quicker her mind seemed to work over the old gossip, the greater her ache for herself and her father. Christmas. It's only a day, she told herself. A random day that had been assigned far too much significance. And yet it still seemed the centre of her life, and her father's. The beginning of everything, and somehow, the end of everything too. Oh, for God's sake, she was crying again. What was wrong with her? She could feel the young woman watching her.

"Are you okay?"

"I'm fine," Juliette said.

"Funny fine that makes you cry," said the young woman.

Juliette turned to her with a little start.

"Christmas is hard." The young woman spoke gently. "Christmas. Birthdays. Looking forward, looking back. Wanting truth more than at any other time."

"Yes," said Juliette. She dug for a tissue in her pocket, and brushed at her eyes. "Maybe that's it."

"Truth finds you, you know. Eventually. Sometimes it waits till you can meet it halfway. Till you're ready to understand it." The woman was silent for a second, then gave a gentle laugh. "Listen to me. For someone who wasn't talking I'm pretty profound, hey?"

The bus shuddered to a stop and the young woman started. "Oh, this is it. I've got to go. Goodbye, Juliette. Happy birthday. Happy Christmas. Look for miracles." She smiled, Juliette felt, into the middle of her. "For you and your dad."

She gathered her coat and scarf, picked up her bags, and rushed after the one other passenger getting off. Juliette peered out the window to a cluster of lights that didn't seem to actually be lighting anything. No recognizable buildings. Where were they? How on earth had the woman known to get off here? Juliette hadn't heard an announcement. They couldn't possibly be where she needed to be, Juliette thought, if it was the stop before her own. The wind dropped momentarily and as the bus started to pull away again, Juliette caught a glimpse of a sign through the blowing snow that confirmed her fear. She strode to the front of the bus. "That woman who just got off, that young woman—it's not her stop, it's the wrong stop."

The bus driver turned to her. "Woman?"

"The young woman who just got off. You've got to go back for her."

"A man got off. Sergeant Blakemore."

"Behind him. I saw her. I was talking to her. She

can't get off here, it's the wrong stop. And with this weather, she'll be lost."

"I'm sorry, miss. I don't know who you saw, but maybe someone stood up and sat down again. No woman got off."

"But..."

"Miss, I've got to drive. I can't argue with you in these conditions, okay? Please sit down."

Juliette went back to her seat, where she felt the light, earthy scent of the young woman lingering. She looked around. People were staring at her, then looking away. She peered back out into the storm. What was it she'd said to Juliette? *Funny fine*. And then happy birthday. Had she told the woman it was her birthday?

The bus pulled past the ancient pumps at the gas station near home, and as always, her dad stood leaning against his truck, waiting. Juliette allowed herself to be pulled into his tight hug; his old overcoat smelled of cold and snow and firewood and smoke—all the winter smells that told her she was home.

"Hey hey! Happy birthday, my grown-up girl. Twenty-one. Legal everywhere now! D'ya feel different?"

"Nearly. Not yet. It's tomorrow, Dad. I feel..."

He held her at arm's length for a moment, then stepped back to scrutinize her. "What? What's going on? Are you alright?"

"I'm...fine." And Juliette started to cry once again, her father looking first surprised, as people pushed around them to get their bags, then worried.

"Fine, eh? Funny fine."

"That's what she said too."

"Who said?"

"This woman on the bus... Come on. Let's go home. I'll tell you on the way."

Juliette climbed up into the front of her father's pickup, where Saxon their border collie waited, barking deliriously in welcome, turning round and round on the seat before settling heavily on her lap. His welcome distracted them both for a moment, but as soon as they were easing onto the old highway, her father said, "So. What's up?"

Juliette told him about the young woman she'd sat with, and her concern that she'd been mistaken in her stop.

"I'm sure she's going to end up stuck somewhere she has no clue about, with no one to help her—it's Christmas and everyone's indoors, or gone, and the bus driver didn't even notice her! I couldn't believe it. He just drove off, leaving her there in the snow. I wish—"

"You wish what?" Her dad was fiddling with the wipers, adjusting and re-adjusting their speed as they struggled against the heavy snow.

"I wish we could drive back and see if she's okay."

"Juliette, look at these roads! And we're expected for supper, Janice will be keeping it warm—you were so late as it is. I'm sure that woman's fine."

"But—"

"Come on, love, let's go home, eh? Get out of this?"

Juliette looked out the window. Her father was tired and anxious—she knew he hated driving in weather of any sort.

That night, curled up in her favourite armchair in front of the wood stove, with a dog at her feet and a cat on her lap, and a mug of her father's homemade eggnog in her fist, Juliette's own comfort only seemed to heighten her concern. He pulled the door tight behind him to stop the draft from the hallway and then put another log on the fire.

"I hope this doesn't go on for too long," He settled opposite her. "I don't relish being snowed in yet."

Juliette remembered what the woman had said about loving being snowed in. "Do you ever like it?"

"Once in while. In January. When there's no work I can do anyway. When I've got a good book from Christmas—did you get me a book?" He smiled at her.

"Dad..." Juliette began, knowing her dad had a hard time refusing her.

"Juliette, you are not getting me out tonight. I'm sorry, love, but I'm not going to shovel the truck out now only to do it all over again in the morning. And I'm not driving anywhere in this."

"In the morning then?"

"What?" Her father looked at her, pretending he didn't know what she wanted.

"Dad. Will you take me back in the morning?"

"Juliette..."

"For my birthday present."

He sighed. "Put like that, what can I say? But not if it's storming still, agreed?"

"Agreed. Thanks, Dad." She didn't know why she couldn't let it go. "Maybe she spoke to the RCMP guy and everything is fine."

"RCMP guy?"

"The man who got off ahead of her. The bus driver knew him. Sergeant...something. Sergeant B—It was a B name."

"Blakemore?"

"That's it!"

"That'll be my buddy Jack. Keeps his horse at Joanie's. Lives in Kemply Rocks with his mother. They might not even get ploughed to Kemply Rocks by tomorrow. Well, we'll see I guess. Okay, we'll go, but you have to help dig out. Deal?"

"On my birthday?!" She grinned at him.

"On your birthday." He grinned back.

Morning came with not even a whisper of the biting winds of the night before. The fresh snow was light and featherlike, easy to shovel, thought Juliette with relief as she pitched load after load away from the truck. The plough had been through, and the roads were shining as the sun and the Christmas Eve traffic began to warm them. It didn't feel a particular hardship to be knee-deep in the fluff that sparkled as she threw it from her shovel.

"Look at you!" Her father appeared, holding a coffee mug. "All this before breakfast!"

"Come on, then," she said, leaning the shovel against the house and climbing into the truck.

"Oh, I see. No breakfast?"

"You can stop at Tim's."

He sighed a pretend sigh, got in with his mug, handed it to Juliette, and pulled on his belt. Turning to her as he started the truck, he smiled. "Look at you," he said. "I haven't seen your cheeks that kind of snow-pink for years."

The roads were good, salted already, and then ploughed and sanded as they got closer to Kemply Rocks. They parked at the gas station where, Juliette realized now, the bus had stopped last night. She headed inside.

The young attendant hadn't been there the night before and couldn't help. There were houses close by on the main street, he said, and perhaps if the woman was lost she'd have gone there. Juliette thanked him, then joined her father back at the truck.

"It's a gorgeous little place, isn't it?" she said.

"Lovely," he said. "But not a metropolis."

They'd yet to see a soul, apart from the young man in the station. Nothing moved in the deserted street except an orange cat, delicately picking its way through the snow towards a tiny café and bakery flashing an incongruous neon *OPEN* sign. The café, a white-steepled church, a convenience store, and a tiny hardware store constituted the business section of the main street. Beyond the church, tiny, brightly coloured houses chased each other with a kind of inevitability to the dead end of the main street, where the spectacular view—and stomach-churning cliff drop—was protected by a thin guardrail.

Juliette and her dad's were the first tracks down the street. They stood silent, peering over the edge and out to the Bay of Fundy, not raging now, as it must have been the night before. Only the faraway lapping of the sea against rocks, and the occasional cry of a gull, broke the stillness that enveloped the tiny village. Far below them, at the bottom of the vertiginous drop, the grey-blue ocean was frosted with floating chunks of ice and snow. A path led off from one side of the rail; a snaking, treacherous zigzag down the rockface to the beach below.

Her dad broke the silence. "Come on, love."

Reluctantly they turned, and as they did, a door banged shut nearby.

Her father shaded his eyes, squinting into the light at the nearby row of houses. "Huh, it's Jack. Jack!" he called, "Hey there!"

The man, carrying a shovel down the short drive on the last-but-one house on the street, glanced up, grinned, and waved. "Good grief, Ray, what are you doing in this godforsaken spot! On Christmas Eve!"

"Godforsaken? You live here, boy!"

"That's how I know! Hey, have you time for a coffee? My mother makes the best coffee ring on the shore and it's just come out of the oven—Christmas treat. You've saved me from shovelling." He planted the shovel in a snowbank near the front door, opened it, and waved them in. "Bless you both! Come on in. We'll have a catch up!"

Inside, the tall, broad-shouldered man grabbed her father by the hand, pumping it and grinning before turning to Juliette. "And this will be Juliette. Good lord. The last time I saw you, you were—well, never mind. Says more about me than you. But look at you." He turned to her dad. "Right beauty, Ray." And there was more there, Juliette saw, that he didn't say, but something in his eyes made her wonder how long he had known her dad.

"And properly gown up, at last," said her dad. "Twenty-one today."

"So, cake is perfect! Mother?" Jack called as they looked around the coziest cottage Juliette had ever seen. Warm and cluttered with books and shelves full of knickknacks, and cats everywhere: on chairs, the sofa, and the books—Juliette discovered there were only three, a mother and two kittens, but it felt like many more. She felt like she'd been drawn into a storybook illustration of Grandma's house. And then, when Jack's mother came through to greet them, wiping her hands on her apron, the white-haired woman with the rosy cheeks and beaming smile, half her son's size, confirmed everything Juliette felt about this morning: they'd stepped into some kind of magical fairy-tale snow globe.

"Welcome!" said the woman. "How lovely to have visitors on Christmas Eve. We don't get too many surprise guests here, so it's a treat!"

Introductions were made, and Minnie—she really was called Minnie—bustled around settling them in, getting tea things out, introducing the cats, who, groaned Jack, ruled the house. Juliette sank into a corner of the sofa and was immediately joined by the smallest of the three. She felt, watching Jack adjusting the logs in the fireplace, completely in the right place.

Her father was finishing his explanation, begun outside, of why they'd struck out for Kemply Rocks this morning.

"...and as it was all she wanted for her birthday." He grinned at her. "I thought, well, that's a nice economical present, and here we are. But we didn't find anything, did we, love?"

"No. I don't know if I expected to."

"Well," said Jack, "I was on the bus—"

"Oh, of course —" Dad said.

"—I've just put it together," said Juliette. "You're Sgt. Blakemore, the RCMP officer the driver told me about?"

"That's right. I'd left my car at my partner's place. But I didn't see anyone else get off when I did."

Juliette's face fell. "It's so odd. I saw her. She even turned to me before she left. She was so lovely and so, so..." She found herself lost for words. Their connection had been so unlike anything she'd experienced before. She turned to her father, who was watching her with pity. She started again. "I'm sorry, I..." Then stopped and stared, confused, at the shelf beside him.

"Oh..." She rose from her seat and crossed to where her father sat, his easy chair pressed against a crowded bookshelf. She stood in front of it, her breath coming quickly, as she tried to understand what she was seeing.

"What's the matter, Juliette?" Her dad turned to her. "What is it?"

"Where did—are these yours?" She turned to Minnie.

"Which, dear?"

"These. These."

Sitting with some rusted antique wire spectacles and a selection of sea glass was a pair of red baby-sized shoes with a sparkling button on each strap.

"Oh, well yes. Though, like all my treasures, they were found."

Juliette gently picked up the tiny shoes and cradled them.

"Where? Where did you find them?"

"Well, it's some time ago now—a long time ago. Twenty years, maybe. They are precious though, aren't they?"

Juliette couldn't find her voice; didn't know what she'd say if she did. Minnie looked to her son and then Juliette's dad before addressing Juliette.

"It was a day like today, actually. I remember that as clear as clear. In fact, it might have been today—or not *today* but Christmas Eve—all those years ago... I remember because Jack's father used to take the village children out in our wagon the day before Christmas Eve. We'd go with the horse every year to get our tree, and they came for the ride. But that year was like this, a terrible storm that kept us indoors for the day. You couldn't see a yard in front of your face. So he'd had to wait, hoping he could still find a tree and get it set up by Christmas Eve. And he did! The next morning was like this, glorious after a terrible night. They all went off together and came back with a beauty."

Juliette was listening intently, staring at Minnie. Her father was watching her.

"Where did you find these?" Juliette pleaded, holding up the shoes.

"Well..." Minnie looked a little uncomfortable. "I often take a path down to the shore—"

"The one at the end of the street?"

"No, no, that path's far too steep. There's another way, very sheltered, at the other end of town, which brings you down to that same beach. I loved, I still love, to walk there. See what the tide brings in. So that day, when they'd all gone, I popped out for my little airing. I found those little shoes on the beach."

"In the water?"

"No, dear, in a little...oh, what would you call it, a little cleft of sorts, I guess. That rock face has breaks and jagged bits that stick out. These were sat sticking out of the snow on one of those clefts. Still seems odd. In a little bag, wrapped in tissue. Not even wet."

Juliette took the shoes back to her seat and turned to her father. "I've seen these. I've seen them before."

"What do you mean, love?"

"I saw them yesterday. I held them. Like I'm holding them now. The woman, the beautiful woman who walked off the bus into the snow, she bought these for her baby daughter. She told me. She told me. And she had a watch. Did you find that?" Juliette turned to Minnie, who was looking at her son, confused.

"No," said Minnie. "No, I didn't, but I didn't find these today, dear. I found them—"

"I know," Juliette interrupted. "Dad—"

"Juliette—love, don't be rude."

"I'm sorry, I'm sorry, but I need to know. The woman, she showed me these shoes and said she couldn't bear to be away from her baby because she was so interesting. She'd gone to Halifax to shop for her baby and her husband. She said *funny fine* to me when I started to cry. I don't know why I cried..."

Her father's face was moving, moving the way she remembered from years ago when the sadness had made the dust in the sunlight shift like waves of heat above a desert.

He crossed the room and knelt next to her chair. "Juliette, love. Please."

"She said truth finds you, sometimes you have to meet it halfway. She said she'd bought the watch for her husband, it had a compass on it, because she said she was afraid she'd lose him in the fields, that he had no sense of direction. She said—"

Juliette's father's face was white, and he was reaching to his back pocket, his hand shaking. He took out his wallet, and Juliette felt so tender, so sad for his hands, gnarled and suddenly so old.

"What did she look like Jule? Was she—" He was carefully unfolding a tiny creased photograph.

"—She was dark. Dark hair. Beautiful," said Juliette. "Greenish eyes. Like...like mine," Juliette discovered. "And a voice like..."

Her father's hand shook as he handed Juliette the one photo he had kept of Frances, and said, "A voice like colours."

Juliette stared into the face of the young woman who'd sat and laughed with her from Halifax, who'd stepped off the bus last night, and twenty years ago. The beauty with eyes like Juliette's, who'd lost her way in a vicious storm and an unfamiliar, sharp-edged landscape. The warm and loving mother who had said to Juliette as she left the bus, Happy Birthday, Happy Christmas.

And, look for miracles.

Juliette turned the photo over and read her mother's words, written so many years before, but singing now, untying the knot of sadness pulled tight for twenty years:

You are my North, my South
My heart, my eyes, my mind, my mouth,
All find their way to yours
The compass of our love will pull me ever
Ever closer, back to you

Frances

Winter Sky

(for Albert Thompson, 1917–2004)

He loved the stars for the stories that lived in the deities' shapes.

Lonely under the endless prairie sky, they were company for him. Given a choice, he'd trade the sod roof of his father's homestead shack for the pin-pricked canopy that let in light from another larger universe. The infinite, spreading out and beyond, like rings in a tree that grows forever, always one outside pressing on the others.

He knew those ancient Greeks who danced now above his head. Ptolemy's *Almagest.* All manner of creatures, and folks like his own, who boasted large, extended, complicated, and vindictive families. Whose feuds sprang, like the perennial rows fertilized with shit, from the soil of northern Alberta: this and this and this is mine. Or ours. My daughter's not for you, or your son, or your brother.

He knew the chaos that erupted at Andromeda's wedding to Perseus. He understood Cassiopeia's ambition for her child: the vanity that left her revolving in the sky, forever. First upright, then hanging, her immortal beauty mocked: laundry pegged to a line.

He wondered if Andromeda could have averted the crisis, taken her mother aside and said, "You promised you wouldn't today."

His mother woke him long before the sun was up to walk to school, only the constellations for company. Orion: hunter, lover. A *Boy's Own* hero. Canis Major keeping the coyotes at bay.

The biggest boy in the middle class, he went early to set the fire; to throw back drifts from the door and windows to let diluted winter light filter into the small, high-ceilinged room. All the heat clinging to the rafters, the air thick with wood dust from the stove as the minus-thirty backdraft lifted ashes from the day before.

He'd climb the frozen drifts by the front door, Mount Robson now, to push the snow off that peak when he swept the straining overhang of the porch.

Soon his classmates would line up beneath it, pushing and tumbling to get out of the cold; pulling the cardboard lining from their boots to dry; unwrapping faces swaddled in every shade of lamb. Relinquishing hot potatoes from their mittened hands to keep warm under the lip of the stove, wanting them now and having to wait for lunchtime when the flesh will be dried out and floury and crunchy. They'd wash them down with rust-tinged water: snow, melted in the well-dip coffee can, two tea bags between fourteen students and a teacher. Elixir, with the teacher's drop of condensed milk. But later then, for all of them, nothing to warm the cold trudge home.

He never waited for lunch to eat his potato. As soon as the stove was lit, the floor swept, the desks tidied into rows waiting exact and parallel, he'd sit. Luxuriate in the quiet warmth, uncluttered with farm responsibilities or God, who took up so much space, or sibling jockeying; he'd bite into the soft white fruit, and scan the shelves of books for what was next.

Astronomy. Astrology. Mathematics. Geometry. Physics.

With the low moaning of the wind as music, his ballet of guilty equations on the chalkboard were the only scratch marks on the stillness. Pressing the precious-white just enough. Never breaking what his teacher bought with her own money, pulled one at a time from a box of ten, one for each month, working the stick till it was only a stub.

A nub. A chip. Dust. Deliberately, tender and meticulous, he covered the board. Motes riding low sunbeams through the windows landed on the tips of his workboots.

Then carefully, he'd swipe it off with snow and finally, his sleeve, leaving it fresh. As though the numbers, full of possibility, had never danced white, constellations on a blackboard sky.

Acknowledgements

This book has been growing for a while: starting with stories commissioned by the CBC in 2010 and 2011 ("Bowls of Cheer" and "December 1945"), right up until the spring of 2025, when the newest stories, "Winter Sky," "The Thing of It Is," and "The Wheel of Cheese," arrived.

Working on all these stories has been a gift of memory, reflection, and memorializing for me, and such a pleasure to craft and re-craft both the old and new tales. Because of these stories, I spent time with my parents, both gone for over twenty years. I thought deeply about my relationships with my siblings, and the way we grew up, and why. Writing is revelatory, and so much has been revealed to me: I hope, though, readers will enjoy these not for my discoveries, but for how mine prompt yours.

My mother, Alice Watson/Thompson/Williams, and her parents and siblings inspired "Bowls of Cheer"; my beautiful stepfather who brought my mother and my brothers and me the gift of a wheel of cheese and unconditional love; my father, Albert Thompson, who loved the stars and the Greek gods and mathematics, is celebrated in "Winter Sky." Other stories are based on what they shared; some on tidbits friends gifted me (thanks to Dr. Michael Cussen for the germ that grew into "The Compass" and to Raymond O'Neill and Juan Goya for the Christmas Eve long ago that was the spark for "A Goat's Christmas Carol"); some I had the fun of just making up. I loved combining a group of builders I've worked with on numerous renos into one wise carpenter, but nodding to each of them. I was grateful to play in the shallow water of my dreams and splash about in my own story, trying to balance truth and longing.

Enormous thanks to Peggy Hemsworth for giving my confidence as a writer a kickstarting boost. While a producer at the CBC Radio in Halifax, she encouraged me to write some of the early stories for broadcast. Then, I was fortunate to meet Christopher Palmer, an extraordinary Halifax composer who scored

"December 1945" and "The Compass," turning these stories into movies for the mind with his beautiful music, to be performed with my dear pals in the Blue Engine String Quartet. Performances of "Bowls of Cheer" and "December 1945" were broadcast by the CBC over a few Christmases and, along with "The Compass," have been performed many times. The Quartet's love of the stories; their collaboration, musicianship, and creativity; their generosity; their ability to laugh and cry as if for the first time, have been such gifts to me. I hope you know that, Jennifer Jones, Anne Simons, Hilary Brown, Alexandra Bates, and Margo Aldrich.

I'm so glad these stories are out in the world now, in a beautiful holdable book, with gorgeous illustrations by Bee Stanton. So many thanks to all at Nimbus/ Vagrant, and to my terrific editor, Whitney Moran.

And thanks so much to my first and most patient reader—my husband, Ed Thomason, and my son, T. Thomason, who inspires me every day with his vision, tenacity, and purpose.

Joanne Corkum

Writer, director, and activist Shelley Thompson is based in Wolfville, Mi'kma'ki. Thompson's first directorial feature (*Dawn, Her Dad & the Tractor*, 2021) screened internationally and won the 2022 Nova Scotia Masterworks Arts Award. A multiple ACTRA award-winner, Thompson continues to work on stage and screen while building her writing, directing, and producing credits. Her first documentary series, *Translations*, aired in 2025. She is the creator of THE DAWN FUND, which supports trans futures in Atlantic Canada. *Winter Sky* is Thompson's second book. Her debut novel, *Roar*, was nominated for the Margaret and John Savage First Book Award and the Forest of Reading Evergreen Award.